3-24-18

To Briar

From your - new friend,

James A. Misino

MW00743968

CONTENTS

Part I

The Deadly Decision

The beginning of our saga finds us on a small island located several hundred miles off the Eastern coast. Unknown to most of the world, a small band of scientists are working together to create a missile device called the Atomic Particle Reaction (A.P.R.) capable of cleansing the pollution in the earth's atmosphere. Seven (7) scientists are now discussing the launching of the A.P.R. They are on the tiny island which they named "Hope". The time is 3:00 P.M. on the afternoon of July 3rd, 2057.

Dr. Lawn was first to speak. "Gentlemen! I still insist that it is way too early to launch the A.P.R. We must test out the possibilities of its reactions numerous more times before we send it up. Why, the consequences, if we have miscalculated, would or could be disastrous for our entire planet."

Dr. Peters countered, "Nonsense! We've tested the A.P.R. for 5 years now. It's proven nothing but success. You know as well as we do, Doctor, the situation of our planet. Ever since Meteor Angelus exploded on the outskirts of our atmosphere back in March of '52,

1

our air has become more and more polluted, year-by-year. At this rate of increase, the germs in the air will have us all dead by the turn of the century."

"Agreed," Lawn said, "but we still have a little bit of time left before any danger of death occurs. I say let's use the time constructively and make 100% sure of what we are doing."

"We _are_ 100% sure, as far as I'm concerned, piped in Dr. Carnes. "Dr. Lawn, you're the very one of us which designed the A.P.R. Without your knowledge, we never could have done it. Most of its success would go to you."

"Or, its failure," said Lawn. "I'm just too uncomfortable about it."

Then Dr. Peters jumped in. "Excuses, excuses. The longer we wait, the closer we are to death. There may not be any time later on. There are 7 men and women here. I say, let's put it to a vote. The majority wins and that will settle it. Do you have any objections to that, Doctor?"

"I guess not," said Lawn. "It looks like I have no choice but to go along with the vote."

Dr. Carnes agreed. "You're right about that, Doctor." (So, the 7 men and women begin the ballot. After about 10 minutes, all the votes were in.)

Dr. Pole tallied the votes. "One vote _for_ the A.P.R. launch, two votes _for_, one against, three for (a few moments of hesitation, then)

As you can see ladies and gentlemen, the final 3 ballots are _for_ the launch. 6-1 in favor. Now, our only question is, When?"

"You fools," Lawn shouted. "All of you. I regret the day I ever designed the A.P.R. We really don't know what we're fooling with. What happens to mankind now is out of my hands and into yours. God help us all." (At that point, Dr. Lawn angrily leaves the room. The day and time of the A.P.R. launching has been set for the next day, July 4th at precisely 3:00 P.M. That night, Dr. Lawn is having a discussion with Dr. Peters outside the laboratory.)

"Here we are. On the eve of what could be a new beginning or possibly the destruction of all mankind," Dr. Lawn sighed.

Dr. Kathy Peters chided, "Don't be such a pessimist, Doctor. Two hundred eighty-one years ago, tomorrow, America acquired her independence. We merely plan to give the world, you can say, its independence from pollution. The A.P.R. would not only clear up the pollution caused by Meteor Angelus, but also all of earth's other natural pollutions. Imagine what we'll be able to accomplish."

"I'm afraid to. The imagination can extend from the innermost part of peacefulness to the outermost part of horror. Doctor, Kathy, listen to me," pleaded Lawn. "It's not worth the risk while we still have time for more testing."

"Look Frank, tomorrow night at this time, you'll realize what a great thing it is that we have done. We'll all be remembered," answered Peters.

"I'm sure of that," said Dr. Lawn. "We'll be remembered throughout history, one way or the other, provided of course there will _be_ a future for us to _be_ history."

Dr. Peters cut off the exchange. "Good night, Doctor. We've got a big day ahead of us tomorrow, so try to get some good rest."

"Yes, Kathy," Lawn silently told himself. "_We'll_ see you tomorrow."

At that, everyone went to bed. 7:30 the next morning, everyone woke and prepared for the big day. After several hours of work, the 7 men and women had a quick lunch, then made final preparations.

Dr. Pias announced, "It's 1:25 and we're right on schedule. The only problem we could run into would be the Thermal Blast. We must make sure there's enough force to propel the missile just above the earth's outer atmosphere. Unless it reaches that distance, it won't explode and release the Sabonite Particles into earth's atmosphere."

Dr. Hond added, "And, as we all know, we _don't_ get a second chance. Once the A.P.R. goes up, we'll have the Secret Service and Armed Forces of every government breathing down our necks in a matter of hours. So, we'd better make sure the 3:00 launching will be the one."

As the 7 Doctors frantically prepare, no one notices Dr. Lawn slip out. The time is now 2:33.

"It's 2:33 and we're all set for launching," Dr. Tad declared. In just 27 more minutes..." Just then, Dr. Tad is interrupted by

4

something she sees and hears. "Good God, what's that coming our way?"

"They look like military ships," shouted Hond.

"And they look like military copters," added Peters, pointing to the sky.

"We've been betrayed!" cried Dr. Tad.

"Well, it's no secret by whom," said Carnes.

"Where's the traitor now?" Pole asked.

Dr. Pias answered, "There he is, down on the beach, meeting with the military."

Dr. Peters hollered, "Quick! If we hurry, we can still launch the A.P.R., but we only have minutes. _Let's hurry!_" So, the 6 men and women go to their respective stations and work as quickly as possible for 7 people.

Meanwhile, down at the beach, Dr. Lawn frantically meets the Army landing copters. "Hurry up. This way, he told them."

"Are you Dr. Lawn, the one who radioed us?" the lieutenant in charge barked.

"Yes, yes, but please, we haven't much time. If we don't stop that launching, we may not have to worry about who's who." So, Dr. Lawn, the Army Lieutenant, and dozens of armed soldiers head uphill, toward the lab.

The lieutenant shouted, "There's going to be a lot of explaining needed. What the hell is that?"

"Oh my God," cried Lawn. "They have the A.P.R. activated. We only have a minute or two to stop them. (on the inside of the laboratory)

Inside the lab, the computer counted down the clock: "60 seconds to Blast Off, 59, 58, 57, 56, 55, 54…"

"Just a few more moments till history is made, Peters exclaimed with a big smile."

"We'll still have to wait 15 to 20 hours for the full results," cautioned Pias.

Just then, Dr. Lawn and all the soldiers burst in. "Quick! The only way to stop the A.P.R. is by blasting all the computers to smithereens," he screamed."

"No! Stop!" shouted all the doctors. As the gunfire begins, there was mass confusion in the lab. In the process of destroying the computers, all but Dr. Peters were shot down and instantly killed. Peters rushes up to the main computer circuits located on the balcony of the lab.

"Good Lord! Dr. Carnes, Dr. Pias, Dr. Pole, Dr. Hond, Dr. Tad, all dead. What have we done?" cried Lawn.

The computer keeps on counting… 28, 27, 26…

"WE HAVEN'T STOPPED IT YET," roared the lieutenant. "24 SECONDS LEFT."

"Of course. The main computer circuits upstairs." Dr. Lawn quickly rushes up to the balcony where he encounters. Peters. The two then begin to struggle.

"STOP! It's mankind's only hope," pleads Peters.

"_Let go_, you fool!" counters Lawn.

Just then, since Kathy is a blackbelt, Lawn grabs a paperweight and is about to smash her on the head, but hesitates from fear of killing her. At this point, Kathy pushes Lawn helplessly to the floor.

In the background, the computer continues: "3, 2, 1, Blast off. Atomic Particle Reaction is now in flight. Thank you. Have a nice day."

"Dear Father in Heaven," sobs Dr. Lawn.

"You crazy fool. I oughta shoot you down where you stand," retorts the lieutenant.

"By mid-morning tomorrow, you'll be thanking me, as well as my associates, my dear associates, whom _your_ men slaughtered," replied Peters.

Turning to Dr. Lawn, the lieutenant asked, "So what do we do now, Doctor?"

"I imagine explain this whole thing to the President. He'll have some explaining to do, too, to the other governments of the world. Then, we can only wait, hope and pray."

"Remember, Doctor. This is Hope Island," said Peters.

The Lieutenant angrily fired back, "As for you, Dr. Peters, you're under military arrest. At least until further orders."

After a Presidential closed meeting, and all governments have been informed, the usual accusations and threats were given. But in the end, everyone realized that there was nothing that could be done except to wait. So, the world waits. Meanwhile, the lieutenant has been instructed to stay on the island with the 2 doctors in case they might be needed for any reason. All the other soldiers returned to the States, leaving a passenger boat for the three.

"It's 1:00 in the morning. I think it best that we get some rest," suggested the lieutenant.

"Aren't you afraid we might try to leave while you're asleep, lieutenant?" asked Peters.

"What's the purpose? Neither of you would get very far. Besides, there's no place you could hide, either. Now get some rest," he said. So, the three enter dream world, hoping for many more such nights to follow.

At 7 A.M. the three arise to greet a new day. The doctors talk while the lieutenant radios in to the States.

Excitedly, Dr. Peters exclaims, "Well Frank, we should know any time now. By the way, thank you for sparing me the burden of having to see a head surgeon."

"If you're referring to me not smashing your head with that paperweight yesterday, you're very welcome. After a split moment's thought, I realized that even if I did hit you, there wouldn't have been enough time to shut down the main circuits, anyway."

"Does that mean you would have struck me if you felt you had a chance at stopping the launch?"

"Probably not. I wouldn't want your blood on my conscience, especially since there _is_ half a chance the A.P.R. could succeed as planned."

"And it will. You'll see," replied Peters.

"It's a funny relationship we have," said Lawn. "We've known each other for 12 years, and sometimes being friends interferes with our business life."

"Sometimes there's a very fine line between business and what's sociable. It can be a difficult line to see."

Just then, the lieutenant rushes into the room. "What's the matter?" demanded Peters.

"I've tried _every_ frequency on _every_ channel possible, but I get no response from anyone, anywhere."

"Jesus, I hope…" said Dr. Lawn.

"Nonsense!" said Peters. "I know what you're thinking. If anything had happened to the world, then why are the 3 of us still unharmed?"

"I suppose you're right," answered Lawn. "Lieutenant, I suggest we head back to the States as soon as possible. It would be the only way to find out what's going on if you can't reach anyone by radio."

"Agreed! The two of you get whatever you need and we'll leave as soon as you're ready."

In 15 minutes, the 2 men and Kathy board the boat and head back toward the States. While traveling, they become very uneasy over the fact that they still cannot reach anyone over the boat's radio, even as they close in on the shore.

It's mid-afternoon now as the boat cruises into New York Harbor. As they draw near, they become aware of the fact that there is no movement of any sort from their view. Finally, they dock at the downtown port, only to be greeted by shock.

"Disserted! The whole damn city looks disserted. Where the hell is everybody?" cries the lieutenant.

"I don't know, but why would the city be disserted? There couldn't have been an evacuation because we would have received some messages on the radio back on the island. Also, there's no sign at all of any disturbance whatsoever," Peters replied.

"Exactly. Which leads us to believe even further that the cause of this has something to do with the effects of the A.P.R." said Lawn.

The lieutenant suggested they make use of the daylight and check out as much of the city as possible.

"Do you think we should separate, to cover more ground?" asked Peters.

"Probably not," answered the lieutenant. "Until we know what we're up against, it's best we stay together."

As the three begin their search of the big city, they scour the majority of it, enough sun still with them as they are able to start a vehicle in the street with no problem at all. Unfortunately, their search brings them no fruit, as building-after-building, block-after-block, mile-after-mile, they find nothing but an empty city. Everything appears to be eerily normal, though. Stores were still open; food vending carts still in the streets; vehicles still had their keys in them, all as if everyone had just abruptly got up and left somewhere. Something so important that people even left their money in cash registers in all the stores that were checked. Nothing different from the norm of life, except _no_ people, or _any other_ form of life. Attempts to reach other people through some of the most powerful radio systems in the world also proved to be futile. Finally, as darkness approached, the 3 decided on a neutral location to try and work things out. At 9:15 P.M., they gathered in front of the 42nd Street Library, the largest in the world.

"We really did do something to the human race, didn't we?" Lawn said.

"It just doesn't make any sense," Peters replied. "If it were our doing, they why weren't the three of _us_ affected?"

"I don't know. I don't know," repeated Lawn. "I don't know the answer to anything anymore. What I _do_ know, is that I'm scared shitless."

The lieutenant added, "and being out here in the dark and quiet streets doesn't help the matter any. Let's spend the night in the Library. We can try to figure this whole thing out tomorrow, in the daylight."

"Sounds like a good idea to us," chimed the doctors. "Let's get the heck in there." Once inside, they were able to turn on the lights since most generators in the city were still operating.

"There. That's a whole lot better, now isn't it?" said Peters.

Looking around, and then facing the lieutenant, Dr. Lawn asked, "Are you thinking what I'm thinking?"

"It depends. What are _you_ thinking?" he answered.

"If we go to the back files of the news, maybe we could find some clue as to what happened," he said.

"Good idea, Doctor. Shall we try it?" Then they all went to the back files and started to check the back issues of the newspapers. But, Dr. Lawn noticed the headline of a paper on the floor.

"Doctor, lieutenant, come over here and take a look at the headline on this paper."

Astonished, they read "The Deadly Decision, the end of all mankind. This will probably be the last story this or any other reporter will ever write. The fate of all mankind was decided today when the A.P.R. II was launched at precisely 3:00 A.M. this morning."

The lieutenant declared, "That doesn't make any sense at all. How could they have found out so quickly? Also, the A.P.R. was launched at 3:00 in the afternoon, not in the morning. And, what's this about an A.P.R. II? I just...."

"That might explain part of it," exclaimed Lawn, pointing to the newspaper. "Take a look at the date on that paper."

"July 5th, 20... (pause) 2064. Good Lord. What does all this mean?" asked Peters.

"I'm not quite sure yet, answered Lawn. "But, one thing for sure, we've found ourselves smack in the middle of a nightmare, one that we created ourselves, and God help us to get out of it."

The three stared at one another in disbelief and horror. Is this the end of the nightmare, or just the beginning, they wondered?

Part II

The Decision Made Clear

Dark shadows seem to pass over the two doctors and lieutenant. All night long, they searched all the back files to figure out what had occurred, from July 2057 to the last known date, July 5th, 2064. The truth to many questions had now become clear, although many mysteries still remained. Dr. Peters and the lieutenant listen on as Dr. Lawn dictates into a recording device.

"So now we know through study of past newspapers the consequences the A.P.R. had on all living creatures, or at least partial effect. According to history, the A.P.R. back in 2057 was successful. The pollutants in the air began to clear up almost instantaneously. Within a matter of weeks, earth's air was completely purified. It was truly a time for rejoicing. Centuries of polluted accumulations cleansed in a matter of weeks. But, as history shows, man usually has rejoiced for short periods of time. This was no exception. It was only 5 years later, in August of 2062, when the second solar system Probe came back to earth. When it entered our atmosphere, something caused it to explode, releasing deadly gases accumulated from other planets. The combined deadliness of the gases with earth's naturally polluted air from volcanoes and such, mixed in with man's own polluted creations, would cause major fatality rates by the year 2067. I think at this time, I should mention a funny point. The papers mention the death of my 5 colleagues who were shot down in the lab on Hope Island, but goes on further to say that Dr. Peters and myself disappeared with Lieutenant Crane of the U.S. Army on the morning of July 5th, 2057. A nationwide search was conducted for us, but we or any clue of our whereabouts were never found. By the end of the year, all hope of ever finding us was given up. No further information of any relevance concerning Dr. Peters, Lieutenant Crane or myself were ever mentioned again. Also, there were no further mentions of the A.P.R. until November 16th, 2062. It seems that the only solution man could find to save themselves from death caused earlier by the Probe explosion was to construct another A.P.R.

It's beyond me why mankind, with all its incredible technology, would have to resort to the A.P.R. II. Couldn't they realize that fooling with such a potent missile could eventually cause more harm than good, especially since they didn't have a deep enough understanding of its design? I guess, to them, progress was worth far more, even at the risk of total destruction, than regression of technology at any pace. True, the original A.P.R. was successful, and did perform a miracle, but in my memoirs, and I have to assume they found them since that was the only way they could have recreated the A.P.R., I stated the high risk factor of launching any device such as the A.P.R. for at least 25 years. That is the time it would take for any remaining Sabonite particles to disintegrate without any more trace. Obviously, it didn't matter what the risk, it should have been used only as a last resort at the end of 2066 if no other solution had been found. On April 10th, 2063 construction began on the A.P.R. II.

A group of 8 scientists led by a Dr. Marlow, swore to have it completed by April 1st, 2064. This would allow time for 3 testings, April 5th, May 15th, and June 25th. If successful, the actual launch would be July 4th, 9:00 P.M., marking the 7th anniversary of the A.P.R. I wonder whether they were able to follow my formula correctly, or if it was their ineptness that ultimately led to A.P.R.'s malfunction. Whatever the case, Dr. Marlow and his associates worked feverishly to remain on schedule. To the delight of the government, construction was completed 13 days ahead of plans, on March 18th of 2064. The 3 major tests were kept on the original set of dates, and with ease each one went smoothly. With a sense of surety, launch would definitely take place as planned. The world would wait eagerly for the day. If only she knew what lay ahead.

Finally, the day came. The hours passed. But, for some reason, launch took place 6 hours after the 9:00 P.M. set time, so it wasn't until 3:00 A.M., the morning of the 5th, that it actually departed. A flaky excuse that there was a faulty wiring in the blast control was given to the public, but Dr. Peters and I knew differently. A mistake like that under so much preparation by 8 scientists would be impossible. Anyway, that's irrelevant now, since we may never know the truth.

The final paper, that of July 5th, 2064, states that to the horror of the world, just hours after the A.P.R. II exploded, the Sabonite particles apparently became crystalized for some unknown reason, and in turn began to absorb all of the earth's air supply. Experts predicted that there wouldn't be enough air left by midnight to keep an ant alive. The world became frantic and desperate for a solution, but one never came. Finally, the proposed savior of mankind, its liberator, the A.P.R. II, turned out to be man's final destruction. It seems like man will never again have to worry about progress; we've gone as far as we'll go.

Unfortunately, there are still questions that plague us, such as if all life died of suffocation, then _where_ are all the bodies? And, for a world of suffocating people, there wasn't much havoc, which is hard to believe. The _most_ important question is _how_ in the stars above did Dr. Peters, lieutenant Crane and I wind up 7 years into the future?

"It could be our present, you know," said Dr. Peters.

"What do you mean, our present? Yesterday we were in 2057. Today, we're in 2064. By my calculation, that's a 7-year difference," answered Dr. Lawn.

"You're right. It is a 7-year difference. But again I ask, is it our future?"

"I don't get you," exclaimed lieutenant Crane. "What's the difference. Seven years is seven years."

"Not quite," Dr. Peters replied. "The difference is, if one goes from one day to the next and covers a span of 7 years, even though it only seemed like 1 day, 7 years would still have actually past. Consequently, it means that it is now their present, along with everyone else, not their future. You see, one would be in the future _only_ if _more_ time has elapsed than actual time one has lived."

"Then you're insinuating that we've been hibernating for 7 years?" asked the lieutenant.

"I'm not insinuating anything. I'm merely giving my conjecture about what has happened to us. I find it hard to believe that we just floated into the future," said Peters.

"And I find it hard to believe that we've been _snoozing_ for 7 years," replied the lieutenant.

"Listen, lieutenant, you may be wise as a military man, but as far as science goes, you get an 'A' for '_ass_'," said Peters.

"Look here, Doctor. I ...."

"The two of you! Please. We're not going to solve our problems _this_ way. We must _search_ for the answers. Also, we should find out _exactly_ when we are. That newspaper was _last_ dated July 5th, 2064. We could actually be days or weeks ahead of that. It's of course obvious that we can't be too far ahead of that because nothing around us has aged very much. Food is stale and moldy, but not to the extreme. Other items do not have much dust accumulation," said Dr. Lawn.

"And, by observing the stars last night, I know we're in July. Putting together what you just said, that means we're still in July of 2064," added Peters.

"Now we're accomplishing something! What practical use it'll have for us, I don't know," observed the lieutenant.

"At least it's a start. I don't know about the two of you, but I sure as hell could use some rest," concluded Lawn.

Dr. Peters agreed. "Me too," added the lieutenant, "but I suggest we wake around _noon_ so we can still have plenty of daylight to use."

"Fine. I'll tell you one thing I'm relieved about," added Lawn.

"What's that," Crane asked.

"We're sleeping while it's _light_." Slumber engulfs our friends as they escape their problems shortly by way of sleep. Hours pass as the hands of time foretell the hour to be 10:15 P.M. in the evening as Lieutenant Crane first awakes; then after coming to life, runs in a frenzy to wake up the 2 doctors.

"What's the matter?" they both shout.

"Look for yourselves," barked the lieutenant. "Look at the shape this place is in. Also, it's dark outside. What's going on?"

As they wipe the sleep from their eyes, they're struck with astonishment. Everything around them has molded, accumulated dust inches thick, and become full of cob webs as if a decade had passed.

"What the hell's going on here?" shouted Peters.

"Quick. Let's check outside," said Lawn.

19

They do, and to their amazement, the city of New York seems to have mildewed as it _time_ itself has taken some sort of strange revenge on her.

"Everything looks like it's aged about 10 years. Am I dreaming or what?" asked Crane. "_We_ still look the same, so what's going on?"

"Good question," answered Lawn. "I tell you one thing. Our nightmare is getting worse by the minute, and so are all these blasted mysteries."

"It's getting too dark," said Crane. "I'm going to run across the street to that hardware store and see if I can find us some lanterns and/or flashlights. None of the generators obviously work anymore."

Nervously, Dr. Lawn agreed. "Fine," he said, "but hurry up, Okay? It's pretty creepy out here."

"I'll just be a minute. I assure you," as he runs off to the hardware store.

"_Nothing_ seems to make any sense anymore," declares Peters.

"Nothing except _maybe_ your theory about time. Maybe somehow we _are_ hibernating through all this. It would explain why we haven't aged, either. We both know they've been working on suspended animation," explained Lawn.

"But how could it _happen_ to us? If we … Shhh, did you hear that?" cautioned Peters.

"No. What? What was it?" asked Lawn.

"Almost like voices….. They're gone now."

"You're beginning to give me the creeps too, Kathy," said Lawn. Just then, an icy cold shiver ran down their spines, almost as if something in the air scratched its claws down their backs.

"What's keeping the lieutenant? Maybe we'd better check on him," said Lawn. As they cross the street and enter the hardware store, the cold shiver accompanies them. They search and search the dark store, yelling for Lieutenant Crane, but no reply comes except a breeze of cold wind from outside.

"There's no way he could have left except through the front door, and he didn't leave _that_ way," Peters said.

"Then where is he?"

"Who knows now?... Let's get out of here. I get a bad feeling about this place."

"I've got a bad feeling about everything," said Lawn. In the street, the two are haunted by the deadly quietness around them.

"What are we going to do from here?" asked Peters.

"Get the hell out of here and head toward Washington, D.C."

"Why there?" replied Peters.

"Because that's the only place I can think of that might have some answers on file," said Lawn.

"Fine, fine. Anywhere but _here_." The two of them try to locate a vehicle in working condition, but have absolutely no luck.

"DAMN IT!", shouted Peters. "We'll never be able to go anywhere with all this junk. It's almost as if we're now pioneers of this city..... This cold, clammy night air doesn't feel natural.

Something's wrong. Something's very wrong. It's piercing right through me. A horrible chill."

"Also, it seems to be getting darker; abnormally darker," added Lawn.

"Almost as if something was trying to close in on us, just like it did on poor Lieutenant Crane," said Peters.

"Come on Doctor. Let's not let our imaginations run wild on us."

"We don't need much imagination for it to run wild under _these_ circumstances…. WHAT'S THAT?" cried Peters.

"WHAT'S WHAT?" shot back Lawn.

"Listen! In the wind. Voices, like before. Don't you hear the voices? Ever so faint, but they're there."

"I don't hear any… WAIT! I do hear voices. They seem to be passing in the wind. Wait! Now they're becoming stationary," said Lawn. "They're like whining cries."

"Cries for what?"

"Cries for…. HELP. Listen!"

Faintly in the blowing wind, the voices grew louder and louder and then faded out, saying: "Help us. Help us. Ooh we are lost. We are not alone. PLEASE HELP US. HELP US. Help us. Help us. Help us Help us."

Horrified, the two now stood alone as the cries in the wind ceased, as if crushed by something wishing to silence their lonely pleas. Only a cold chill does the wind offer now.

Dr. Peters breaks the silence: "My God! What have we done? WHAT HAVE WE DONE? WHAT? WHAT?" she shouts frantically.

"Calm down. We've gotta get control of ourselves. CALM DOWN!" begged Lawn.

"I can't take this anymore; not another second." Dr, Peters then starts running without direction down the street with Dr. Lawn in pursuit.

"Doctor, come back. Kathy. Kathy. Come back! Come back!" pleaded Lawn.

"Good Lord, forgive us."

"Kathy, please! Stop! Stop!"

"NO! NO! We've created a HELL. That's what we created, a hell on earth. DO YOU HEAR ME? A HELL; A HELL; A…" Just as Dr. Peters turns the corner of 42nd Street, her voice becomes silent. Seconds later Dr. Lawn rounds the same corner, but only confronts shock as he finds an empty street. The wind and whatever else has now taken Dr. Peters too, as Dr. Lawn stands bewildered and stunned.

In the blowing wind, Dr. Peters faint voice began to become audible: "HELP US. HELP US. PLEASE HELP US. PLEASE HELP US. Please help us. Please help us."

Hours now pass as fatigue befalls Dr. Lawn. His sleep is not a peaceful one as all his sub-conscious can think of is death, murder, loneliness. Finally, dawn awakens him, but this dawn is not like most others. It's a gray, hazy one. The once-great island of Manhattan

23

now seems like a prison island of lost souls. Unsure of what to do, Dr. Lawn walks down the lonely, deserted streets making his way to the harbor, where he, Dr. Peters and Lieutenant Crane once docked their boat. But now, their boat lies crumbling apart in the waters from age. Yes, again while Dr. Lawn slept, somehow years passed by - this time about 20, and to him it feels as if it has indeed been 20 years since he last saw his friends. He now gazes out into the ocean, almost as if expecting an answer back from the sea. His only response, though, is the brisk air splashing drops of ocean upon his face. None of the drops, though, can quench the dryness in his throat. Standing there, he remembers what used to be, tries to understand what is, and fears what will be. Coming to grips with himself, he decides he can no longer go on this way. Guilt, loneliness, and fear have eaten him alive. His options are gone, and soon, so will his life.

He whispers to himself, "I'm sorry. Please forgive me. I have no other choice."

Just then, the doctor hears voices and other noises in confusion behind him. As he turns around, he's astonished to see what appears to be forms of people wandering aimlessly. Forms of people from eras of New York's past, mixed together with those of the present. Even that of what appears to be some type of pre-historic animals. Greatly confused, he begins to walk toward his apparitions or whatever they may be. Suddenly, beneath him, the earth begins to tremble. The ocean begins to rise and the sky darken. Is this the "Last Days" that was foretold in the Bible? No more time to think.

The doctor lurches forward in a terrified manner. Agonizing cries swirl around him. He feels the temperature dropping rapidly. He senses earth's impending doom. He hears pounding waters behind him. He turns in horror.... BLACKNESS; ALL BECOMES QUIET.

Part III

Time Has No End

After what seems like an eternity of sleep and darkness, Dr. Lawn begins to regain consciousness. Once alert in mind, he finds he is in a king-sized plush bed of old design, but in new condition. The room is a huge Victorian type with large windows and what appear to be some sort of outside balcony. As he rises and starts walking toward the balcony, the hallway door opens up and a pleasant looking man in his mid-40's comes walking in wearing 20th century leisure clothes.

"Welcome back, Dr. Lawn," says the man. "My name is Quint Darley. Please call me Quint. I trust you've had enough rest?"

"Yes, plenty, thank you. How long *have* I been resting?" he replied.

"Almost 18 hours. You needed it, though," answered Quint.

"No argument from me there. Would you mind telling me now how I got here and where *here* is?"

"Certainly," replied Quint. "A small group of scientists transported you here via a transporter machine just as you were about to be swallowed by the ocean. You'll see the equipment in a short while. _Here_ happens to be the shoreline off of Boston, Massachusetts. This is an estate owned by four very preeminent scientists of our time and myself, overlooking a breath-taking view, if I might say so myself."

"Boston?" replied Lawn in bewilderment. "There was no answer when I tried to call people in Boston. I'm afraid I have about a hundred questions or so to ask you."

"Understandably," replied Quint. "Shall we go out onto the balcony. If I give you a full explanation, that might answer most of your questions. It might be a good idea, though, to first change into some clothes."

Realizing he is in a robe, Lawn agrees. "You'll find something that should fit you in the walk-in to your right. After you've changed, I'll meet you out on the balcony," said Quint.

"You're right," said Lawn. "It's a breath-taking view." The balcony, as most of the eastern part of the estate, overlooked the ocean crashing upon the rocky cliffs which the estate rested upon. "So, tell me the story, Quint. What's been going on? Also, how did you know of me?"

"Truthfully, we've – meaning the four doctors plus myself – have known of you for years," he said.

"How's that?"

"We have the technology to monitor anyone, anywhere on earth, at any time period we wish. We had been monitoring you and your colleagues for some time now."

27

"That sounds hard to swallow, but then again, so has everything else happening these past days, _or_ years, or whatever," answered Lawn.

"Relax. Let me explain. Back in your world, in July, 2057, your 6 colleagues launched the A.P.R., Atomic Particle Reaction. Unknown to any of you at the time, the thermal blast itself had released some of the Sabonite particles within the atmosphere of the island you 7 were on. Unfortunately, the particles themselves, when exposed to earth's oxygen, not only cleansed it, but affected it in such a way that time and space, themselves, were altered."

"I'm not sure I follow you," said Lawn.

"Let me clarify, then," said Quint. "Your intentions were to send the A.P.R. up to earth's outer atmosphere, where it would explode, releasing the Sabonite particles, which would then encompass the planet and purify the air of pollution caused by the meteor Angelus. That's very fine, except that the Sabonite particles caused an atmospheric disturbance which disrupted the protective element in our atmosphere. This element protects us from becoming intertwined with time and space itself. In short, time and space in your world is coming to an end. Soon in ours as well. It's all merging together, getting ready for total destruction. Your world is almost gone. That was all the forms of past lives you saw right before the quake. They aren't what _used_ to be, but they _are_ what exists in their own time and space. It's just that they were all converging together before all the worlds in your space and time came to complete annihilation. Soon, that same converging will take place in ours," explained Quint.

"You've continually said phrases such as 'your world', 'our world', 'all the worlds'. I don't understand," Lawn said, almost jokingly. "Aren't we part of the same world?"

"To be blunt, NO Doctor Lawn, we're not. Time runs on a continuous basis. Also, so does space. This was part of Einstein's theory. There are many planet Earths, each in its own dimension. Also, there are countless eras of time for each. Under normal circumstances, the time and space of a planet Earth in one dimension couldn't affect the outcome of time and space of Earth in _another_ dimension. They're two separate entities. Only the time within an Earth of its _own_ dimension could affect _that_ Earth's outcome. For example, if you were to go back in time on your planet Earth in its dimension and change some point in its history, when you return to your _present_, the outcome of events would also be changed, but _only_ on the Earth in _your_ dimension. _My_ world in _my_ dimension would not be affected by what you had done in yours. Only someone living in _my_ planet Earth in _my_ dimension could alter history by traveling through time.

"Then when and where am I now?" asked Lawn.

"As I previously explained, you're in Boston, Massachusetts, but no longer on the Earth in _your_ dimension. You are now on _my_ Earth, in a different dimension, or plane if you prefer, than before. The _date_ of my world is May 4th, 1926. If you're confused, remember that the way we progressed and designed _our_ planet Earth would be completely different from the way you and your people did yours. So, if things seem odd to you, this is the reason. Many cities, states and countries have different names. Our histories are different. I could go on and on, but I presume you understand my point."

"I do…. You said you brought me here through a transporter device of some sort," said Lawn, inquisitively.

"Yes! If we had waited any longer, it would have been too late. You would have been killed. As I mentioned before, what anyone from your Earth, in your dimension, does would not affect the outcome of anyone in mine, _normally_. But, because of the A.P.R. _and_ A.P.R. II, now all of our worlds of Earths in all the times and dimensions are crashing together by a chain reaction. The people from the Earth in _your_ dimension have opened a time and space portal that should never have been touched by man. Now, unless something is done soon, there will no longer be any Earth in _any_ time or dimension for evermore."

"Well, what can I do now?" asked Lawn.

"I'm coming to that."

"Also, do you know what happened to my friend and colleague Dr. Peters and Lieutenant Crane? added Lawn.

"Yes," Quint replied. "But, I must backtrack first to explain. After the launching of the first A.P.R. on Hope Island, as you refer to it, the small amount of Sabonite particles that were released there had already begun to alter time, but only in the slightest degree. As the air carried them throughout the island, by mid-morning, the whole area was affected so that by the time the 3 of you had awakened around 7 A.M., you were already thrown into a time disorder."

"Then that explains why Lieutenant Crane was unable to reach anyone when he awoke," replied Lawn. "We were already in the future. But why wasn't the search party affected that searched for the 3 of us? Also, what _did_ happen to the rest of life on my planet Earth?" asked Lawn.

"First off, the search party was affected, but as in most cases as these, the military kept it all hush, hush. Only Top Brass knew about it. You shouldn't be surprised about that, Doctor," added Quint. "That sort of stuff happened all the time on your Earth."

"Is that the reason then why construction and launch of the A.P.R. II was on another island?"

"Exactly. After July 7th, 2057 Hope Island was completely quarantined. Nothing was allowed on _or_ near it. In answer to your second question, concerning what happened to all living things, it began after the first A.P.R. was launched. It exploded, releasing all the Sabonite particles into the atmosphere as planned. Shortly thereafter, the air was purified as hoped. The problem was, it had also started the chain reaction of time and space disturbances. Because it occurred on the outer atmosphere of your planet, it would take either a 40-year period or another explosion comparable to A.P.R.'s for it to reach a level of 30,000 feet and below, referring of

31

course from the point of sea level. It _was_ affecting time and space around your planet to anything above 30,000 feet. If you did a very thorough search of back newspapers, you would have noticed many problems with space shuttles and other aircraft traveling above that height. Unfortunately, your time limit was cut short by 33 years when, at 3:00 A.M. of July 5th, 2064 A.P.R. II was launched. That was the explosive force needed to propel the Sabonite particles which contained the time and space disorder elements to fall below 30,000 feet and reach all living creatures. It spread throughout the waters as well, affecting all sea life as much as land or air. Because of the disturbance of time and space above 30,000 feet, the Sabonite particles from A.P.R. II got caught in between times and dimensions. To your world, it appeared as if they were becoming crystalized. This time, instead of purifying the air, it was drawing Earth's oxygen along with it to other times and dimensions. The people of your Earth didn't understand this and thought that their air supply would be gone within a 24-hour period. This didn't happen, of course, for once the particles fell below 30,000 feet, air was being forced back from other dimensions just as they were taken from your Earth's. By the time people had a chance to rejoice though, the Sabonite particles were upon them. Because of the heavy dosage that fell upon them, all living beings were affected quite rapidly. People were thrown into other times and dimensions as well as some getting caught in between. All other forms of breathing life were also caught. The rest of your planet was affected by progressed aging from time to time, but didn't disappear because it was not actually breathing in the air. Your friends, Dr. Peters and Lieutenant Crane, were caught in a time or dimensional portal somewhere and were in limbo. Only their voices could sometimes be heard in the passing wind. It would have happened to you sooner or later, except for the fact that your planet began to crumble and we had to quickly pull you out and bring you here."

"Then that explains so many mysteries," said Lawn. "Tell me, do you know why the 2nd Solar System Probe exploded back in August of 2062?"

"Yes!" replied Quint. "When reaching Earth's outer atmosphere, it came head on at incredible speed and heat to the floating Sabonite particles. The impact caused an immediate explosion. It had spread quickly with the help of the Sabonite particles, and then just the pollution made its way to Earth's air below 30,000 feet."

Dr. Lawn reacted, "Why couldn't you have brought _all_ three of us here instead of letting my friends get dragged away by this nightmare?"

"We were having extreme trouble with our transporter unit. You see, it was originally designed to transport _only_ objects, _not_ living entities. We really needed more time. The chances were high that you would not have made it, but it came to a point where we _had_ to try or we would have lost you for certain."

"I see," said Dr. Lawn sadly. "What was the reason for the six hour delay of A.P.R. II?"

"Shortly before the 9:00 P.M. launch, the eight scientists had realized that the Sabonite particles might have had something to do with many of the strange occurrences over the past seven years. This bit of information came due to the fact that the testing area for the A.P.R. was already creating strange effects. Pressure brought on by the government, though, forced them to launch against their better judgement. So, launch did take place, at 3:00 A.M. of the 5th instead of at 9:00 P.M. of the 4th. It's too bad, their hesitation was a chance." Dr. Lawn looked puzzled. "What's the matter, Doctor?"

"I was just thinking, if there is a future from *my* original time, and there *is*, since I, Dr. Peters and the Lieutenant traveled there, then that means that *my* period of time that I'm from is *not* the beginning point. We're just following some other time before us."

Quint replied, "Yes and no. Come on, Doctor. I thought you were intelligent. Haven't you been listening to what I've been saying? It makes no difference *which* comes first. Time is a continuum. If you believe in the theory of God, it's very similar. Like God, time has no beginning, and time has no end. So, there cannot be a central point. It always was, is, and always will be."

"If all of this is true, then under these unique circumstances, there's no way we can change the eventual destruction that's about to occur, because time would eventually catch up to the point of the A.P.R. and A.P.R. II. I mean, even if I or someone else went back in time to stop the A.P.R.'s launch, somewhere down the line as history repeats itself, someone *will not* be able to stop the launch, and since

34

it all affects each Earth in each time and dimension, it will be a chain reaction that will still destroy us all," explained Lawn.

"True!"

"Also, since the future has already happened, why then hasn't everything _already_ been destroyed since it's all related together?" asked Lawn.

"Because the future has already solved this problem, so they still exist," explained Quint.

"Then down the time continuum line, the problem _will_ be resolved!"

"Not true!" answered Quint. "History does not repeat itself _exactly_. As you said, somewhere down the line, someone _will not_ prevent the A.P.R.'s launch. Then, time _will_ catch up."

"Then you mean that everyone in the future still lives in fear that it will all or _might_ come to an end at any time?"

"Yes!" answered Quint. "For those who understand this process, that is."

"Then, _what_ in the name of blue blazes can _we_ do to stop this nightmare once and for all?"

"By going back to the beginning," replied Quint.

"The beginning of what?" asked Lawn.

"Right _before_ the beginning of _man's_ time."

"I thought you said time _had_ no beginning _or_ end."

"It doesn't," answered Quint. "I said *man's* time. Don't get confused. Time has always been, long before the Earth and long after it. Man didn't invent time; *only* a way to *measure* it."

"I think I'm beginning to understand now." All of a sudden, a shocking realization hits Dr. Lawn. "*Wait* a minute. If my memory of history is not affected by all this, then I do believe that *man's* history began with a pair of human beings by the names of Adam and Eve."

"Your memory serves you well, Doctor."

In shock, Dr. Lawn demands, "What in heaven are we trying to do here? Are you actually saying to go so far back in time that even Adam and Eve were not created yet?"

"That's exactly what I'm saying," replies Quint.

"Whoa! Whoa! This is *too* much. Don't you think (almost jokingly) that *God* might have something to say about this? Or, let's go a little *further*. How about *Satan*? You know, 'Prince of Darkness' and evil and all that stuff; *he* was there before Adam and Eve, too."

"Please sit down, Doctor," said Quint. "What I'm about to tell you is going to be a lot more heavy on you than what I've already told you."

"*This* I've got to hear," answers Lawn.

"The Bible tells us God created the Earth in 6 days, and on the 7th day, he rested. It also says God gave man three blessings: 1) to be fruitful, 2) to multiply, and 3) to have dominion. This was never realized because Adam and Eve fell from God's grace before reaching the 1st blessing. To be fruitful didn't mean they were supposed to sprout fruit all over their bodies, but rather to grow to a state of perfection through God. This is why 2000 years ago in your world, a man by the name of Jesus Christ said 'You therefore must be perfect, as your heavenly Father is perfect.' He didn't say *good*, or *almost perfect*; he said *perfect*."

"Thank you for the history lesson, Quint, but I really think...."

Almost angrily, "Doctor! If you're to understand what is happening, then I must explain some background. As a scientist, this should be obvious to you."

"I'm sorry," Lawn apologized. "You're right. Please continue."

"Thank you. As we discussed in depth, there are many time levels, but there are only six dimensional Earths. For each day, or time period if you prefer, that God created the Earth, another dimensional Earth was also created. Six days, six Earths, each having the same beginning with a man and woman comparable to your Adam and Eve; each having their challenge of faith, each succeeding except those on your Earth. Their failure prevented them from attaining perfection and oneness with God. Therefore, they were banned from the Garden of Eden. God tried to restore what Adam and Eve had lost through two of their children, Cain and Abel. Unfortunately, they too failed, beginning a long line of failures on the part of man. Oh sure, there were some successes in history, but by then, the evil world formed by Satan was too strong and powerful.

So, in your world, mankind lives in boundless misery, mistrust and war. _Now_ is the time. It _must_ end, one way or the other."

"In other words, you're trying to tell me that the five dimensional Earths are ones that have all reached perfection state?" asked Lawn.

"Just the people. The worlds will, in time. Doctor! We are all living in the midst of God's talked-about kingdom. These are worlds of perfect individuals and families all centered on creating the most beautiful and heavenly existence for all creation possible. You are being given this chance to change the faith of your Earth, and ultimately the faith of all six Earths. Change man's beginning of your world, and all six Earths can live in peace and tranquility for evermore. Fail, and it will soon be the _end_ for us all. Never again can the name of _man_ be uttered upon the lips of God."

"How can you be so sure this is what God wants?" asked Lawn.

"When attaining perfection my friend, you know God's every thought because you are one with him, in mind, heart and body. We _think_ as he does, we _feel_ as he does, we _are_ his children."

"If this is all true, then why doesn't God just step right in and stop all this himself? I mean, he is all powerful and all that good stuff, isn't he?"

"Is it still so difficult for you to understand?" Quint asked. "Man controls his own destiny. God cannot interfere with that. When God created man, he created man with a spirit, and made him ruler of all creation. But, in order to earn that right, man had to have some accomplishment that creation did not have. Otherwise, man would have no right to be Lord of creation. Especially since he was the last creation of God. So, God gave man freedom of choice. The right to choose between good and evil. This, no other form of creation has. They only have instinct, and something within them that automatically drives them to do the things they do. A tree just doesn't decide to grow or not; it does. You'll never see a cow decide not to give milk because it wants to live the life of an eagle. It just doesn't happen. If God takes man's most precious commodity "freedom" away from him, man would be more of a robot or just an animal than a being with a spirit. Man created his world by his choice. If it must change, it must also be by _his_ choice, not God's; otherwise there would be no purpose _to_ man's existence."

"But, _you're_ intervening," challenged Lawn.

"We have the right. Remember? We are men and women created by God, _too_. We've accomplished our responsibilities. We've earned the right to have a say in all of mankind's future, _or_ past."

"Then what exactly is my responsibility in all this?" asked Lawn. "What precisely do I have to do?"

"If you've studied Biblical history well, you would know then that Lucifer was originally an angel serving God. He was actually very trusted and loved by God. It wasn't until after he caused Adam and Eve to fall that he became the Devil, Satan, as we, or should I say _your_ world, knows him as. If Lucifer had never enticed Adam

39

and Eve, then they would have never fallen, and your world, as the other five, would have all reached perfection, as well.... You will have two alternatives. One, to convince Lucifer not to tempt Adam and Eve, or two, convince Adam and Eve to keep God's commandment. If you succeed at either, then mankind's history from the beginning would be changed. Your world would advance centered on God instead of Satan, because there _would be_ no Satan. Lucifer would still be a loved angel of God.... The very moment that success is realized, and God will know, then you will return back to your world and time, but a different man. The one that would have been if man had never fallen. If you fail, at the time God realizes the hopelessness, then in all his tears and sorrow, he must let the inevitable occur. At that point, _all_ will come to an end. Everything, even our spirits, will come to an end because God _does_ have enough mercy than to let mankind suffer in agony for all eternity in limbo and other forsaken realms.... This is it, my friend. It's now up to you."

Shocked, Dr. Lawn asks, "How much time will I have?"

"Under these circumstances, total end of mankind will be prolonged until you either succeed or fail."

"If I succeed, will I keep my recollection of all that had happened?"

"No!" answered Quint. "No memory of man's shameful past will ever remain. Only one of success, joy and the brotherhood of humanity."

"Will Lucifer know what's really going on?"

"Not exactly, but he will know that somewhere in God's plans, you have some meaning and purpose," answered Quint.

"Tell me something," asked Lawn. "According to Christianity, God was supposed to send the messiah again to save our people in my world. What happened?"

"It would have taken place very soon, but man caused time to run out before God could set the conditions for his second son to be born. In a crazy sort of way, you are Earth's messiah now. I'm afraid any other questions you have will need to be answered through your own experiences."

"Please, before I begin this whole thing, I must have a little time to be alone with my thoughts."

"Certainly," replied Quint. Dr. Lawn is escorted outside to the rocky cliffs overlooking the ocean. "I'll return for you shortly."

"Thank you." Dr. Lawn then takes time to search himself and understand what it all means. He thinks about his past life, his friends, family, loved ones, those he may never see again. He thinks about all the pain and sorrow his world has endured. Why did Lucifer do this? The murder, the rape, the lonely and destitute. The poor children who had to bear the agonies brought on them from generation to generation. The senior citizens left out in the gutters for lack of concern. Or the forgotten tramps and hobos given up to the harsh elements of nature, left to rot in the streets. So much for what? Where has man gone, but to his judgement, to his demise.... He

41

turns to the west as the sun begins to bow out, maybe for the last time. He gives a heartening stare at the ocean as the cool wind blows in his face. Above him, he hears the whining of the seagulls as they scurry through the sky. Their instinct seems to warn them of the impending doom and look down upon Lawn, almost as if asking him, "Why? Why had man done this to the creation?" As Dr. Lawn turns away with shame, tears come from his eyes. He knows what must be done. No matter what, he must sacrifice; he _must_ change man's destiny. Whatever awaits him, he is ready now. Quint approaches from behind.

"Are you ready now?" he asks.

"As ready as I'll ever be," answers Dr. Lawn.

"Then my friend, let's go."

They both proceed into the estate and down a long elegant chamber, unlike the gloomy ones he knew of in his world. They stop at a huge carved door. Quint opens it and inside is the largest laboratory and workroom Dr. Lawn had ever seen. Most of the equipment there was completely alien to him as he makes his way around in complete awe. Finally, at the other end, he is greeted by a short, stout man who identifies himself as Doctor Woods and his 3 associates: Dr. Camin, Dr. Tyler, and Dr. Jerome. The two men and two women now enter another room where they sit down at a 12-seat oak table. In a short time, they become acquainted with Dr. Lawn, then go over final preparations for the journey that will decide the fate of all.

"There's time enough to answer just a few more questions," concludes Quint. "Remember, you will understand everything as if in English, for of course there was no English language back then. You'll be dressed in nothing but your birthday suit. If you cannot convince Lucifer of the grave consequences of his actions, then you will be thrown further into the future, one day before the fall of Adam and Eve. That will then be our last hope. Just remember, if you do speak with Adam and Eve themselves, they _are_ all mankind's original mother and father. Two other things _very_ important to remember…. Your world was built on mistrust, hatred and war. You will never gain success using these methods. You _must_ win with understanding, love, and compassion. Lose any of these and you've lost the battle. Secondly, somewhere along the way, you will have to master three tests. After each one, if you pass, you will see a dove fly by, but if you fail any, it's all over."

"Do you know what type of tests?" asks Lawn.

"No, I don't. Only that there will be three, in order to rectify three major failures of mankind's past. I wish I could help you more. Just remember to keep faith, yourself. You may not feel Him constantly, but God will be watching over you. _Don't_ lose _faith_…. Any last questions?"

"Yes," replied Lawn. "Two. I know these other men and women are scientists, but where do you fit into all this, Quint? Also, since you are all in a direct line with God, you might say, then why has it taken you so many thousands or millions of years to get to this point? With God as your guide, it should have been so much shorter."

The five scientists and Lawn proceed towards the transporter chamber. "If man never fell," said Quint, "there would be no pollution or other deterrents to prevent man from living exceptionally long lives. The Bible states your Adam lives to be almost 1000 years old."

"It doesn't answer my questions," replied Lawn.

"It will in a moment. Now, my friend, or may I say brother, it's time for you to face the challenge. There's so much more I would have wanted to share with you, but time no longer permits it. I can feel the air changing. The past, present and future waits for the outcome. If we never meet again, remember, we are of the same, now and forever. Even the end of our existence cannot change what was. Go now my brother," said Quint. Then, all four scientists, Quint and Dr. Lawn, embrace with tears. "Don't forget. Keep faith."

As they entered the chamber, Lawn shouted "*Quint!* You still haven't told me."

"We are advanced beyond your wildest dreams, my brother. I said the year was 1926. It's 1926 A.C."

"A.C.?"

"After creation," replied Quint. "It's only been 1,926 years since our Adam and Eve. Our potential is *boundless*, if given the chance. As for *my* part, I have much at heartistic stake in this…. I am the grandson of Adam and Eve."

44

Part IV

The Final Decision

As the transporter chamber door closes in front of a shocked Dr. Lawn, he bids farewell to a man who has become a close friend of his in only a matter of hours.... He begins to hear a humming in his head, a tingling in his body. The chamber appears to be fading. His legs become weak, then his arms, torso, neck, head. Finally, nothing but a pleasant feeling as he finds himself engulfed in what appears to be some form of white cloud, almost as if floating.

Quint says to himself, "Good bye. Good luck!"

Moments later, Dr. Lawn feels his body becoming stationary. He becomes whole again as the white cloud fades from him. He now stands in the midst of a beautiful garden of open space. A warm sun showers its rays upon him. The fragrance of life is in the air. Peace and tranquility accompany him. As he comes to full realization, he knows now that this must be it. Here is the "Garden of Eden", the beginning of it all. A sense of humility comes over Dr. Lawn as he is humbled to his knees.

He says quietly to himself, "Good God in heaven. I'm here. *I'M HERE!* " Looking at himself, he adds, "They must have done away

45

with my clothes, I see. _Naked,_ as Adam and Eve were when it all began." Then he starts running like a child through the open land, investigating all that he sees. The grass, the trees, the animals, the birds, the sky, the earth. All as it was before man ever had a chance to poison it with his diseases. Yes! The real, true, natural Earth, as it was meant to be.... After jumping into a nearby stream, he notices what appears to be a deer. He springs from the water and heads in its direction, but to his surprise, the deer runs away, frightened. "What happened? I thought that man and animals could relate to one another in the beginning without fear," he whispers to himself.

A voice then startles Dr. Lawn from behind. "Animals are very spiritual creatures. They sense something evil from your past. So do I. I can see you are not of us. You are of our image, but you are not the one intended by the Master. Yet, nothing could be without his knowledge and handiwork. Who are you?" asked Lucifer. "What are you? What is your purpose here? What do I feel from your spirit that brings an uneasiness to me?"

Dr. Lawn is stunned at the realization of who he is talking to. "My name is Dr. Frank Lawn."

"What is this word 'Doctor'?" Lucifer asks.

Dr. Lawn catches himself and thinks, "I forgot, he probably doesn't understand many terminologies. Let's see. How can I make him understand?"

"It means one who saves another from sickness," replied Lawn.

"There is no sickness here, and you are the only non-angelic being here."

"I am a man, Lucifer. I have come from many, many years in the future of this Earth. My purpose here is to save mankind from total destruction."

"You say the future. How far into the future do you speak, and what of this destruction you talk of?" asks the angel.

"The end of all living earthly forms, as well as the Earth, itself. _When_ I don't really know the time period from _now_, since there were only symbolic times discussed in our record book from the beginning of time up to the period of Abraham and Isaac. From that point, it was approximately 4,000 years, but the first 2,000 years could have been millions; we just don't know."

"How does this destruction occur?" asks Lucifer.

Realizing the situation, Dr. Lawn decides it best to completely explain to the angel all that he knows. After several hours of explaining and answering questions, Dr. Lawn has a few of his own. "That should explain the bulk of it. Tell me, Lucifer, Why? Why are you planning to tempt Adam and Eve? Your position to God is one of a loving servant to him. He deeply cares and loves you. What's going through your mind?"

"I have no pre-arranged plan, as you say, to cause my Master's creations to fall from grace. I know not of what you speak…. But, surely my heart does ache, because I am becoming a forgotten servant to the Master."

"What makes you say this?" asks Lawn. "God could never forget you. Why you, Michael and Gabriel were the first three living beings he created. He could only love you more as time goes by, provided of course you _do_ remain loyal to him."

"No! Even now the Master forgets me. He thinks only of his soon-to-be children, Adam and Eve. As each day passes, the Master's love for me decreases as his love for _them_ increases. When they are created, his love for me will almost be non-existent. _Why?_ _They_ never served him as I did. _I_ have been with him for eons. _I_ was by his side through all of his creations. I witnessed the birth of it all. The Master conferred with _me_ about his creations. He said 'Let _us_ create man in _our_ image;' not 'Let _me_' or '_my_ image.'" It is not fair for them to receive everything."

"Incredible!" retorts Dr. Lawn. "It's just like a jealous child who learns his parents are going to have _another_ child. The jealousy swells within him until after the birth, then it reaches dangerous levels. He might run away from home, or do bad things in spite. He may harm the newborn, or live with resentment for years until he even has the urge to _kill_ his sister or brother. But, all these feelings and emotions are usually transferred from parent to child down through the generations, traced all the way back _to_ Adam and Eve. If they didn't have these emotions originally, then _where_ did they come from?"

"Are you inferring that I am a child?" asked Lucifer.

"No! By no means. I'm just saying that your feelings are similar to that of future children, which in many cases also are exhibited by full-grown adults."

Angrily, Lucifer said, "Maybe you forget. I'm the angel of intellect. Do not attempt to treat me as inferior to you and man-to-be."

"I have no desire to do so. You must understand, though, that what you are feeling is only a natural response to your situation at-hand. If you love and serve Adam and Eve faithfully, then God could do nothing *but* love you even more. *You* are being controlled by your emotions. You must learn to control *them*."

"*Again*, you speak to me as your inferior," said Lucifer.

"I am *not* speaking to you as my inferior. I am merely trying in desperation to explain to you why you feel God loves you less and less. The faith of *all* mankind depends on your understanding. It's not a lack of love on God's part, but only a feeling of being left out due to God's attention to Adam and Eve. Deal with it. *Master* it, and you will be given all the attention you could possibly want in time."

"Stop it!" Lucifer demanded. "I have listened to enough. You speak *too* boldly."

"I *have* to!" shouted Lawn. "Don't you realize what is going to happen? We have no time for self-pity right now. The Earth and mankind are going to be *destroyed* unless *you* can change your attitude, or maybe you *haven't* been listening to me. Time is running *out*."

49

"I *do not* care *what* happens to man *or* the Earth. As a matter of fact, it would be fine for man to become non-existent. Then, I can serve my Master as once before, and there will be no other object for him to focus upon, except myself, who rules over Michael and Gabriel."

"Well, I can definitely see man's negative qualities in you, but how they were transferred to Adam and Eve, I would still like to know," said Lawn.

"Go back to where you came from, and let the inevitable happen," said the angel.

"If I can't reason with you, then I must try with Adam and Eve. To quit now would just be insanity. Everything would cease instantly and failure is imminent."

"As I have said before, I have no plans to entice Adam and Eve to fall, but due to the facts you have explained, somehow it will come to pass."

"No!" Dr. Lawn cried. "Not again. Either I will succeed in preventing it, or God will *cease it forever*.... You really can't see, can you? Your feelings toward Adam and Eve will only grow stronger and stronger until you are compelled to *make* them fall. Your selfishness prevents you from accepting what I say.... You're wrong if you think God will care for you any more with man gone. He would only *despise* you more since you were the original cause of the problem. *Please*, I plead with you to re-consider your feelings. Take this chance now. I've had just a small glance of what man and

creation would be like if there is no fall. _You_ could be happy. Man and creation could live in peace and harmony, and _all_ of creation could live in the midst of God. I'm not asking you to give up your happiness or chance for it; just sacrifice it _shortly_. Then, you'll be rewarded a _hundred_-fold. You're a spiritual being. You noticed something strange about _my_ spiritual background when I first met you. _Check_ it out. I'm sure you can see some of the misery and hardships you caused. The horrors and agony of man are limitless. The pain and sorrow not only affected man and creation, but the very depth of God's heart. The evil history of man has created horrors that not even _you_, as Satan, could have dreamed of. _Come on_, Lucifer, _open_ your heart. Accept what _can_ be, if only you give it the chance to work. Man won't be your _dominator_; he'll be your _liberator_. Even a fallen man such as _I_ can see this. Surely, you of such intellect can see what I say is true. _Please listen_ to the cries of countless billions and billions of souls. As Satan, you have no room for logic or pity, or the capability for love. But _now_, there is still hope, still a chance to get through to you." Dr. Lawn then gets down on his hands and knees.

"You humble yourself to me as if you were _my_ servant. Have you no pride of your own?"

"Of course, I do, but if a servant I must be in order to melt your heart, then a servant I am; and my pride, if it must, will have to be cast aside. There is no room for such humanistic emotions now....

51

Whatever I _can_ do, whatever has to be done, I am willing, even if _your_ servant I must be," pleaded Lawn to the angel.

Suddenly Lucifer begins to weaken just a bit. "Maybe, I act too hastily. Perhaps I should evaluate my feelings. If you are willing to bend down on your hands and knees as such, before me, then surely, I can at least listen to my inner self. Please excuse me for now. I must go and confer with myself amongst the lilies of the field. I shall return within the hour."

As Lucifer strolls away, Dr. Lawn's attention is brought to the sight of a dove flying in the sky. He now understands that this was the first of three tests he would be given, and he had triumphed over it. With joy and a sigh of relief, he knows he cannot dwell upon it too long, for two more tests he must pass for complete victory. This, though, was surely a test of the heart. Dr. Lawn realizes he must always be prepared, for anything, at any time…. A short distance away, Lucifer ponders the situation. Spiritually, he knows everything Dr. Lawn says is true, but heartistically he feels unsure of himself. What if he does lose God's love after Adam and Eve reach perfection? At least if he caused the fall, as predicted, he would at least be the center of his Master's attention, even if it were for wrong doings. Then again, the feeling of sincere emotion from Dr. Lawn brings warmth to Lucifer's heart. Perhaps it would be worth it to at least try to understand the meaning of Dr. Lawn's words a little more deeply before affirming his stand by himself. Yes! He will give the matter further consideration. He has nothing to lose….

Meanwhile, Dr. Lawn thinks to himself with an impatient concentration. Looking up at the sky, he thinks "I can only hope I have reached Lucifer in some way. I *must* be making some sort of headway. Otherwise, I would have already been thrown into the future to Adam and Eve. What else can I do to convince Lucifer of his mistakes?....It's amazing actually how handsome Lucifer really was, or is. Evidently, after the fall, he must have accumulated all the sin and evil elements that were created by man and himself. Of course, I don't know what Satan *really* looks like, since I nor anyone else *alive* had ever seen him in his true form."

"You think too loudly," said Lucifer as he approached from behind.

"You *listen* too loudly," replied Lawn. "It's hard to keep thoughts to myself when in the presence of a spiritual being…. Have you thought about our discussion?"

"Since that was the purpose of my brief departure, it would only be logical that I have," Lucifer answered.

"You sound like a Mr. Spock of Star Trek."

Whom is this Mr. Spock you speak of?"

"Never mind," said Lawn. "He was only a fabrication of man in the 20th century…. What conclusion have you come to?"

"I have not come to a conclusion as of this time, but I *am* willing to listen to anything more you have to say. My final decision you will receive before the next sun rises…. Come let us share together all we can, while we are able."

Lucifer and Dr. Lawn walk side-by-side throughout the Garden, in the middle of an area which we know today as Asia. Lucifer enlightens an amazed Dr. Lawn with so much of the Earth's original design, about the stars, space and universe. He explains the creation of all life, the plans, the hopes, the dreams. Dr. Lawn's ears are awakened to incredible information that no man in his world has ever known, except of course for Christ himself. Lucifer then goes on to explain even his own feelings as he practically tours Dr. Lawn around. In response, Dr. Lawn tells Lucifer more of his own life and feelings. He also explains in depth the horror and sorrow of mankind's history. As Lucifer listens with eager ears, a sense of sadness comes over him, knowing that he was the cause of all the misery. The conversation between the two continues for hours as each hour draws them closer together in mind and heart. Dusk swiftly comes, and begins to draw out the stars from the sky. As the sun completely disappears beyond the horizon, the stars now light up the sky, and aura-like colors blend in as if putting on a show. The beauty is breathtaking as no pollution or any other man-made obstruction hinders the view. The brisk clean air only enhances the magic of the moment.

"It's incredible," says Dr. Lawn. "I never realized how peaceful and gorgeous a night _could_ be. The real beauty of nature had been lost, replaced by artificial comforts and high-tech advancements that only create a shroud over our eyes. We believed it was all for the better of man, but standing here now, I wonder if we all would have

54

been better off living the pure, simple life instead of our modern world of technology…. I guess the real problem, though, was not *really* the progress of the times as much as it was the motivation of man, himself…. Yes, I think I really understand. It would have made no difference *how* hard we tried to better our world, until we changed *ourselves* first, everything else was futile. How ironic indeed. Man's quest for survival was ultimately his destruction."

"But not for certain, Lawn. There is still hope. I can feel my Master yearning, crying. My heart still aches, but now for a different reason. I can feel the pangs of my own conscience throbbing away. Knowing what the future had been is miniscule compared to the feeling I receive from *your* spirit. I can *see* the agony; I can *feel* the pain; I can *hear* the cries. The breath of man has not yet been formed, and still I am overcome by the potency of just your spirit, alone. Most repulsive is the knowledge that *I* am the one that caused it from the beginning. Much shame is upon my shoulders."

"It doesn't *have* to be," replied Lawn. "You are *your* own entity. *You* have not done *anything* wrong yet. There is *still* time! If you really feel the way you expressed to me, then *do* something about it. Determine to change *now*, and *all* the future *and* past will change. It will be the way God had originally intended for it to be."

"I hear and understand you, Lawn. I said I would deliver you an answer before the next sun. That I will, but I must use these few hours before to be completely at peace with my decision…. Go, leave me to my solitude now, and when we join again, you will know."

"Very well, Lucifer. I understand. Please remember all we discussed…. One more thing. We shared a lot together today. I can't help feeling connected to you somehow. I can understand you in many ways. I can sympathize with you, but only as *Lucifer*. *Satan* deserves only neglect and hatred. For *him*, there is no hope."

At words end, Dr. Lawn leaves and finds a place to rest his mind. Thinking to himself, he ponders: "I wonder if Kathy (Dr. Peters) and Lieutenant Crane know what's happening? It seems like ages since I last saw them. Then again, it seems like an eternity since the decision to launch the A.P.R. Hope Island, Hah! What a joke. If only we had known back then. If only….." Dr. Lawn then drifts off for a much-overworked mind….

Several hours pass as he begins to regain consciousness. Once fully alert, he paces back and forth impatiently awaiting the return of Lucifer. Then, he hears the bushes moving in front of him as he sees Lucifer come out of them. "*Lucifer*, what have you decided?"

"Doctor! I have great news. I have decided to let mankind and all of creation *GO TO HELL!*"

"*WHAT*? Lucifer, *what* happened?"

"I have realized that it is all man's fault for my suffering. It is also man's own fault for his suffering. *No one* made Adam and Eve fall. They had their choice. It was *their* decision. If they cared and loved God so much, they would have been stronger. If they cared

56

about _me_, they would have been stronger. But _NO_; they gave a shit about _no one_ except _themselves_. Now they can just _rot_ and _you_, too, as well as everything else."

"What made you change? You're talking so strangely. Something had to have changed the direction in which you were thinking."

"_Nothing_ did. Now _get lost_. You have _failed_ with me. Go on to your _last_ chance with the cry babies, Adam and Eve. Now get _out_ of my sight, you sickening example of a man."

"I don't understand your erratic behavior, Lucifer. But, if this is your choice. Then, you're right. I _have_ failed with you." Just then, everything goes black for Dr. Lawn. After an indefinite amount of time passes, the Doctor finds himself awakening again in the same area as he did when first transported to the Garden by Quint. Only the scenery around him has changed. Still as tranquil and beautiful, except the growth around him has greatly matured. He now comprehends that he must have gone into the future period the day before Adam and Eve were to fall as pre-explained. This now means that he has but one day left to change mankind's faith; otherwise it's all over. His next blackout would be his last.... From a distance, he can see the figure of a naked man. He knows instantly that this must be Adam. In awe, he begins walking toward him as the man he sees also does the same. When face-to-face, the first response comes...

"You must be the one called Lawn, who comes from our future _and_ past. We have long awaited your coming. Welcome, my son _and_ father," said Adam.

Astounded, Lawn says, "You know me? How?"

"Lucifer told us of your experiences with him many years ago. He explained all you told him and the reason you would be here during our existence."

"But _why_?" answered a puzzled Lawn. "Why would he tell you all this, feeling the way he did when we last talked? Unless he had a change of heart _after_ I was gone."

"Lucifer felt that your disappearance meant his destiny was surely one as you described to him."

"The way he acted, what else did he expect?" Silence befalls the two men. As they observe one another, the meaning of who each of them are, and what they represent hits them like a bolt of lightning. Tears then fall down their cheeks as an enormous embrace captures the two of them. Unfortunately, knowing that only hours may remain, priority must come first. So emotions have to wait, even ones as deep as these. "Where is Lucifer now?" Dr. Lawn asks.

"He is by the meadow."

"And Eve?"

"Praying in the fields… Is something troubling you?" asks Adam.

"Yes! How could all this misery come about by a simple act of eating a piece of fruit from a tree?"

"Excuse me?"

"You know. The fruit from the tree of knowledge of good and evil. God told you and Eve to eat from _any_ tree you wanted except this one," explained Lawn.

"I'm sorry. Our Father gave us no such command," said Adam.

"Are you _sure_?" queried Lawn. "I'm sure Lucifer told you of the Holy book called the Bible. In the very first book entitled Genesis, it tells of the story.... Then, of course, so much of the Bible was in symbolic terms. I, as a scientist, should have realized the possibility that even the story of you and Eve could have been symbolic. There were so many religions with many different interpretations of each story. The question is, which one is true, if any.... You couldn't be more than 16 or 17. What could you and Eve have done that was so terrible for two young people such as you are? Were you given _any_ type of commandment at all?"

"Yes, we were."

"What _was_ it?"

"We were admonished that until we reach perfection at the age of 21, Eve and I were to have a relationship as that of brother and sister. _After_ reaching perfection and oneness with Heavenly Father, then we would be wed in Holy Matrimony."

"Amazing! A perfect couple developing into a perfect family, society, nation and eventually a whole world of perfected individuals, just as Quint tried to explain to me. But history shows Adam and Eve _did not_ reach perfection, meaning they did not wait to the age of 21 before living as husband and wife, or having a sexual relationship.… with each other. My God! That was the fall. An illicit sexual relationship before it was *meant* to be. That's what made it *illicit*. That's the reason you both were ashamed and covered your *lower* parts as recorded in the Bible. You were ashamed because you transgressed against God with your sexual parts.… Still there are several answers needed. The biggest one being *why*? With only a few years left, why sacrifice *everything*? Also, what part does Lucifer *actually* play in this?... *Wait* a minute. The Bible says *Lucifer* tempted *Eve*, *then* Eve tempted Adam. In other words, Lucifer had sex with Eve *first*, *then* she had a relationship with you, Adam. *That* explains why the Bible calls *Satan* our father, and how the insecure and evil emotions were transmitted through mankind *from* Adam and Eve. They all came from *Lucifer*. So, instead of building a world centered on God through perfection, it began centered on Lucifer, eventually Satan, in *imperfection*. Satan's blood *literally* runs through us. And, ever since, he kept his hold on us, deceiving man throughout history, waiting for the day when he could have *complete* victory over God and man. All because of innocent feelings of loneliness and rejection in the very beginning. That must have driven him closer and closer to Eve, and Eve being so innocent and naïve, fell prey to his advancements which eventually led to their relationship. At *that* point, Eve must have been confused and frightened. Coming to the only physical person she knew and trusted, *you*, Adam, felt pity and compassion for her. After relating closely together, the inevitable happened. The two of _you_ had sex, thus breaking God's commandment and beginning man's origin of sin and suffering."

In deepest sorrow and despair, Adam responds, "_We_ caused all that to happen? Father and creation depended upon us so strongly, and we failed them."

"_Don't_ you see? Adam, this is your chance to amend for all of it. You _don't_ have to let everyone down. The fall doesn't take place until tomorrow. Find Lucifer and Eve. _Protect_ her. Pray to God for guidance. _He_ won't let you down."

"_Yes_. You are right. We _can_; we _will_ change what once was. I could feel Heavenly Father slipping away from me. He becomes distant. It is not the same I know danger is near. I miss Father by my side. _Now_ I will bring him back. _Now_ I will be the beginning of a _new_ glorious world. I must find Eve, now."

"Please do. I have a feeling she is not praying as she told you, but rather, she's out with Lucifer somewhere. Find them, Adam. It's crucial."

"Yes, I will. My heart only hopes that I _can_ change what was, if faith will allow."

"Why second thoughts of victory? Don't lose your enthusiasm."

"I keep thinking of Lucifer. He changed his heart many years ago when speaking with you, but still failure was imminent."

"What do you mean," asked Lawn. "In the end, his final decision was for man and creation to go to hell. He told me to my face."

"You are wrong, Lawn. He was ready to repent. His heart was changed. He was in great agony and sorrow when you disappeared in the Garden that night while he was debating his decision."

"You don't really believe him, do you Adam? He was only trying to deceive you."

"Would it not have been to his advantage then to have remained silent about your meeting? If so, I would have been very confused at your arrival. Also, I could tell in my heart, he _was_ telling me the truth. Back then, we were as one."

"Then what was that scene all about? Was it Lucifer or not? said a mystified Lawn.

"Maybe we can understand together," replied Adam.

"No Adam. Whatever is going on, it's even more important now than ever that you find Eve and Lucifer."

"Very well. We will meet again shortly."

"Good bye for now. Good luck." Adam left to find his objectives while Dr. Lawn tries to figure out what has occurred. He says to himself, "I'm really beginning to believe that it wasn't Lucifer I spoke to that final time. It _would_ explain his erratic behavior and also why he called me Doctor instead of my name. Now that I recall, he used the term God instead of Master."

All of a sudden, Lawn feels an icy cold chill all around him. A repulsive stench that causes his stomach to turn accompanies it. A strong sense of fear and confusion also are present. The sky around becomes gray and misty…. As the Doctor turns around, he is horrified at the sight he is confronted with. What appears to be a man of animalistic deformities beyond human description. His deep-set eyes appear to have some familiarity to Dr. Lawn. As this figure begins to speak in his rusty voice, Dr. Lawn tries desperately to keep his composure.

"You think you can fight me? Now is your chance, you little piece of scum. As Lucifer, I might have listened to you. As _Satan_, I will _crush_ you _dead_!"

Part V

The Final Confrontation

Dr. Lawn stands in utter shock as the figure before him is the representation of every evil element there ever was. In him, the one called Lucifer is no longer. Whatever small shreds of compassion there once were are all smothered away in cob webs left for insect food. For, in _his_ world, compassion, love, sincerity, trust and any other facsimile are non-existent. The only elements present here are those of a darker side. Not even the warmth of the sun's rays can enter. Only cold and destitution survive. But, now more than that must survive. Otherwise, the entity known as _Satan_ will reign forever.

"Say something, you ass," growls Satan. "Otherwise, I will strike you _dead_ where you stand. TALK YOU FOOL!"

Trying to remain calm and in control of himself, Dr. Lawn rebuffs him and says, "I don't think you could do that, Satan, for I'm sure if you could, you would have long ago. Your power is limited here. God has something to say in all this."

"Fuck God! You think God is more powerful than _I?_ You are wrong, little man. He is practically impotent. _I_ have control over all

64

his creation now. People care *only* about physical things. God has been forgotten after his puny attempt to save man through his spoiled son Jesus. *I* controlled the minsters and preachers of your time. They speak of God, but only know of me. They know of *one* lord, which is *my* creation. *MONEY!* If that fails, I will control him by his dick. Anything for a quick screw. *Right?* If *that* does not get him, I have a *million* other delectables to snag him with. From the very first moment Eve fell with me, I *knew* God's almighty plan was doomed to failure. Adam, Cain and Abel, Noah's family, Abraham's mistake, Jacob's brother, the Egyptians, Moses' failure, Israel's failure, John the Baptist, the Roman Emperors, King Solomon, high priests, John Booth, Hitler, Stalin, Breshnev, you name them, good or bad. *I* had control one way or another over them or their actions. I had planned for communism to wipe out the free world, and ultimately destroy themselves. But, thanks to you, my dreams of total oblivion will take place much sooner. When all fails, and the Earth is no more, I will be sole ruler over the universe."

"What do you mean, *universe*?" replied Lawn.

"Man was supposed to be the center of the cosmos. Since Adam and Eve, God and I have been battling for dominion over man. He who wins, will also have dominion over the cosmos, as well."

"But if you win, there *will be* no more Earth, man *or* spirit of his to have dominion over."

"You don't understand. I don't give a *fuck* about man, *or* the Earth; *only* supremacy of power over God and his creation. Man and the Earth are only my tools to help me acquire this. Once I win over man, I don't give a shit what happens to him or the Earth."

"Then was it _you_ I spoke to and _not_ Lucifer that final time?"

"Of course, you idiot. It was also _I_ who sent you to this day, _not_ the failure of Lucifer. By doing so, Lucifer then believed that even his change of heart was meaningless, and that he was destined to fall with Eve. So, you can see that God is powerless against my actions. He could not stop my intervention. Once Lucifer falls with Eve, it will all be over for you and pitiful mankind.... Of course, there _is_ an alternative."

"And what's that?" asked Lawn, suspiciously.

"Even though man and the Earth would have little meaning to me after my victory over God, still, it would be a small reward if I could keep man alive and continue dominion over him. As you might say, it would be rubbing it in God's face. _This_ I would enjoy."

"So what do you want from me? And, I know there's something."

"I can prevent the destruction of man, but I need your cooperation."

"Really?" Lawn replied. "This I have to hear."

"Whether it be for good or evil, as long as man exists, his choice or decision always affects the outcome. In _this_ case, there was an instant in time when if you had done differently, _I_ could have intervened and changed history. I can _still_ change history if you take a different course of action when given the opportunity once more."

"Which is?" asks Lawn.

"With under half a minute left before launching of the original A.P.R., you were engaged in a battle with your friend, Dr. Kathy Peters. At one point, you were about to smash her head with a paperweight, but hesitated long enough for her to push you out of the way. *If* you had just hit her without hesitation, you would have had enough seconds left to shut down the main computer, resulting in the AP.R.'s launch being cancelled."

"So, you're saying you can give me that chance again?"

"Yes! But this time you must not hesitate. Kill her. Then, I can change history, and mankind can live."

"What about the pollution caused by Meteor Angelus, and also....?"

Angrily...."I SAID I CAN CHANGE HISTORY *IF* YOU DO *YOUR* PART! Don't worry about the rest," shot back Satan.

"*Why* should I give *you* the chance to rule over man when *I* can stop you *here* in the Garden?"

"*TWO* reasons. One, because if you *do not*, I have *no* further need of you and I will ANNIHILATE you instantly." At this, Satan stares firmly at Dr. Lawn and causes him to fall to the ground in great pain and agony. Moments later, it passes. "Secondly, *you*, Dr. Lawn, would be second *only* to *me* in almighty *power* and *supremacy*. That is right. *Stand*, Doctor, and feel only a *taste* of what you would be capable of."

Dr. Lawn stands up and feels a surge of energy flow through his body as nothing he had ever felt before. As he turns to the fields and concentrates, everything begins to die and whither as if the hand of death itself passed over them. A few more moments of concentration, and they are all restored again. Another burst of energy causes the sun itself to begin to darken; moments later, it too is restored. For 5 or 10 minutes, Dr. Lawn is astounded with feats of God-like powers he has acquired, and tests them out in many more fashions. There seems to be no limit or bounds as to what his new powers can do, except for where it would concern Satan. Here, they meet their match. Still, Dr. Lawn can hardly restrain himself with all the inner emotions and sense of almightiness. _Then_, as quickly as it came, it is taken back.

"Only a taste, Doctor; only a taste. Do as I ask, and all you were, _plus_ some, will be yours. You could travel the heavens if you please, and outside of myself, _no one_ would be greater than _you_. Mankind would _live_ and owe it all to _you_. _You_ would be their messiah, their God. You could create your _own_ world. Create many. You want peace and happiness in a world? _Make it_ yourself. Your potential would be limitless. So would the possibilities. Just say the word 'Yes', and you will have the chance over again. _Kill_ Dr. Peters, and in the long run, she and everyone else will be saved. Say 'No' and you will _die_ anyway, being unable to prevent what _will_ be."

As Dr. Lawn's mind is cluttered with everything that has happened to him, the feeling of power he had shortly is too strong for him to refuse. Besides, he would also be saving man, as well.

He eagerly tells Satan, "Yes! Yes! Give me the chance."

As a hideous grin comes over Satan, he lifts his arms in the air, thunder and lightning streak through the sky, and the Earth trembles. A sharp pain hits Dr. Lawn as he blacks out. Moments later, he finds himself on a familiar beach.

"Where the hell am I?"

"Are you Dr. Lawn, the one who radioed us?" asks Lieutenant Crane.

Now realizing where and when he is…. "Yes, I am. But please, we haven't much time. If we don't stop that launch, it's all over for all of us."

As once before, Dr. Lawn, Lieutenant Crane, and dozens of armed military men head uphill toward the lab.

"There's going to be a lot of explaining needed…. What the hell is that?" the Lieutenant barks.

"The A.P.R.; It's activated. We only have a minute or two to stop them."

In the lab, the computer counts down: "60 seconds to blast off, 59, 58, 57, 56, 55, 54,…."

"Just a few more moments until history is made," proclaims Dr. Peters.

"We'll still have to wait 15 to 20 hours for the full result," reminds Dr. Pias.

Just then, Dr. Lawn and all the soldiers burst in. "Quick! The only way to stop the A.P.R. is by blasting *the main computer circuits*," cries Lawn.

Before Lawn can explain the location, hoping to avoid the deaths of his five colleagues, the soldiers begin to fire.

"NO! STOP!" cry all the doctors. But, as before, in the confusion, all but Dr. Peters are shot dead.

"Good Lord! *Not again*. I thought I could have prevented it this time," says Lawn.

The computer continues: "28, 27, 26,...."

"WE HAVEN'T STOPPED IT YET; 24 SECONDS LEFT..." shouts the lieutenant.

While running up to meet Dr. Peters, Lawn declares, "Of course not. We need to stop the main circuits upstairs here."

"STOP!" cries Peters. "It's mankind's only hope."

"Out of my way, you fool!" Dr. Lawn then grabs the paperweight as he did once before, only this time determined to put an end to Dr. Peters' life. As he lifts his arm up to come crashing down upon Dr. Peters' skull, all of a sudden *time* seems to stand still, and through his mind and heart, many thoughts and feelings occur. "What am I doing" I'm as bad as *Satan* himself. Who do I think I'm fooling? I'm doing this *only* for *myself*, not for humanity. I'd be condemning God, man *and* creation to Satan's subjugation to who knows _how_ long before God could stop him again. All for _what_? A meaningless power. Something which is not mine to have in the first place."

Then, in his distant mind, he hears the sad, terrifying cries in the wind he heard before. "HELP US. PLEASE BEFORE IT'S TOO LATE. PLEASE HELP US. HELP US. HELP US."

"Yes! I will. I will," said Lawn. "I _MUST_ STOP IT _NOW_! I _MUST_ GO BACK TO THE GARDEN!"

Then, turning to Peters, _time_ again begins as Dr. Lawn throws the paperweight away with great force. "_NO! NO!_ I will _NOT_ KILL YOU!"

"3, 2, 1, blast off. Atomic Particle Reaction is now in flight. Thank you. Have a nice day," concludes the computer.

Lieutenant Crane then walks up to Dr. Lawn and shouts at him, "You stupid son of a bitch. _Why_ the fuck didn't you _kill_ her while you had the chance?"

A puzzled Dr. Lawn asks, "Lieutenant! This isn't like you to use such language."

"_Shut the fuck up!_ It's over! Satan set this up for you to _kill_ Dr. Peters this time. But, you _failed_."

Stunned, Dr. Lawn responds, "Satan _never_ had any intention of giving me any powers, _or_ of saving man and creation, _DID HE?_"

"Of course, he did," the Lieutenant replies.

Just then, Lawn looks out the lab window and sees a DOVE fly by. "You liar! If I would have killed Dr. Peters, _that_ would have been the end of everything. That was my second test; a test to denounce material things, such as the power I thought I would have received."

From behind the soldiers, Dr. Peters and even the supposedly dead doctors begin to surround Dr. Lawn.

"You're a loser either way. Your own friends turn against you," said Crane.

"These aren't my friends. Nor are you Lieutenant Crane. You're all a bunch of phonies, just like this whole scene."

"That's right," said Crane. "Angels to be exact. _Satan's_ angels." As he speaks, each man begins to turn into a demonic angel. "Unfortunately for you, _time_ has expired. You will _never_ return to the Garden to save mankind. Surrender _now_, and we will spare you an agonizing death."

"_Go back_ to hell, where you came from. I _haven't_ got the time for you."

"_THEN DIE!_" shouts one insulted and infuriated angel. And, with a great force of his hand, he bolts an energy spark that hurtles Dr. Lawn through the window and onto the beach. Bleeding and hurt badly, he struggles to his feet as he sees the demonic angels almost gliding towards him. In pain, Lawn says, "Where should I go? What should I do? God, where are you? I need help! Please, help me!"

As he limps toward the water, the angelic being who portrayed Lieutenant Crane quickly glides in front of him. The angel that attacked him cries out to Crane, "Hey creep. I'll give you a fighting chance, creep. I'll fight you hand-to-hand. If _you_ win, you go back to the Garden. If _I_ win, it will obviously be all over with. What do you say, creep?"

"It doesn't look as if I have too many options…. These other parasites, they won't interfere?"

Looking at the other demonic angels, he nods, and they all fade away. "Now, it's just you and me, scum-bag."

"Your language could use some improving," quips Lawn.

"So will your fucking face when I'm done with it," the demonic angel retorts.

At that, the angel lunges at Lawn as the battle begins. With each blow from the angel, a hurting Lawn retaliates with all his strength. Kick after kick, punch after punch, blow after blow, each painful strike draws more and more strength from Lawn. It seems as though the angel never tires. Maybe because he is a spiritual being, but to Dr. Lawn, he is definitely physical enough. As the fight ensues, the two gradually back up into the jungle area still scratching and clawing, blood and sweat mingling together. Deeper and deeper, they go back until they come to a deep pit about 10 by 15 feet wide. For a moment, the fight halts.

"You see, God doesn't give a fuck whether you die or not. If he did, surely he would have helped you. Your strength is almost gone. Blood, sweat and disappointment cover your face. Are you ready to give up yet?"

"Not yet, you son of a devil." Then Dr. Lawn lurches forward with all of his remaining strength, grabs the shocked angel, and with power and authority flings him down the pit to his fate. A deafening scream roars from the depths of the pit to the skies above. Dr. Lawn then looks to the sky to see if there be a dove, but none fly, thus knowing he still has much further to go. Moments later, he again finds himself back in the Garden, still dark and gloomy as he is greeted by Satan.

"You look like you've been through hell and back," he says to Lawn.

"You're *not* going to win," fires back Lawn.

"You do not seem to understand yet just who it is you are dealing with."

"I don't *care* *who* I'm dealing with at *this* point," shouts Lawn. "I've come *too* far now to let anything or *anyone* get in my way."

"I see. Maybe *I* should just give up to *you*."

"That would be nice."

Laughing loudly, "You pitiful little shit," said Satan. "Throughout history, most men have ignored me, and those few that did not thought that they could resist or defeat me….. Mankind is sooo foolish. I have had a relatively easy time handling him. A *dog* would be more worthy prey for myself."

"Yet it took you all these years to get *this* far. You do yourself an injustice, Satan. If we're such easy prey, *why* is it taking you so long to eliminate man?"

74

"If it were man alone, I already would be reaping my rewards of victory. Unfortunately, God has been helping man along. But _now_, God might as well be _dead_. His grace and forgiveness is _no more_. His once-mighty powers are _gone_. He is _old_, _weak_ and _feeble_. He has long grown tired of assisting man. _Weary_ is His mind, no longer can He think rationally. At last, _cold_ grows His _heart_, for those that were once His beloved children are now mine. They mock Him, laugh at Him, use Him _only_ when convenient to do so. He is forgotten, except for when someone needs something of Him. You know, "Oh God, please help me. Oh Father in heaven, just help me get this job. Oh God this. Oh God that. And, if it is not granted, they say 'I _knew_ you couldn't do it,' or 'Now I'm _sure_ there is no God.' How fickle man is. God no longer has a place in your world, and definitely not mine. It is now time for Him to sleep, _eternally_. He is out grown, obsolete, and in less than an hour, Lucifer will fall with Eve. Thus, mankind will also be obsolete."

"Less than an hour?" says Lawn, struggling to move in pain. "I thought I was sent here a whole _day_ before the fall. What happened?"

"So sorry. That was _my_ doing. Remember, _I_ was the one who sent you to this time period, not God. So, I figured 15, 20 hours would not make that much of a difference for you. (laughing) That only goes to prove my point further. God _will not_ help you. He _cannot_ help you. He was hoping for one of His own miracles, but at last, His miracle well has all gone dry. _No more_ bag of tricks. No more Moses; no more Elijah; no more Jesus. THIS IS IT. THIS *IS* THE END! THE LAST DAYS HAVE COME AND MANKIND *BLEW* IT! IT IS ALL *MINE* NOW. *DUST* IS NOW *YOUR* FUTURE!"

"It *can't* be true," responded Lawn, frightened and confused. "God *couldn't* have abandoned man. He *can't* be powerless. *What* was the meaning of it all?"

"The *meaning* was lost years ago. *FORGET IT*, and accept *now* what is to be."

"NO! I WON'T There has *got* to be a reason for this. It's *not* too late. It's *not* over yet," demanded Lawn.

"*IT IS!* ACCEPT IT!"

"*NO!* I can't accept it, because I *KNOW* there is still *HOPE*. If not, the end would *already* have been, but I'm *still* here."

"You *keep* forgetting. *I* am in control now, and *I* opt to wait till Lucifer falls with Eve. *Then*, I will allow your puny lives to return to *oblivion*."

Dr. Lawn turns and struggles to make his way across the field. "I *must* find Adam, or Eve, or Lucifer. Time's running out."

"IT HAS ALREADY RUN OUT FOR *YOU*!"

Lawn ignores Satan and continues on his way.

"STOP! IT IS OVER!" shouts Satan.

Lawn still continues....

"I SAID *STOP*, YOU FUCKING SON OF A BITCH!"

As Dr. Lawn still continues his bloody path, a now furious Satan disappears and reappears directly in front of him.

"NO ONE BUT NO ONE IGNORES *ME* WHEN FACE-TO-FACE. NOT EVEN THE SHIT CALLED GOD! YOU THINK MY SLAVE THE ANGEL HURT YOU BAD? BEFORE *I* FINISH WITH YOU, YOU WILL THINK *HE* GAVE YOU A MASSAGE. NOW STOP! *I SAID STOP!*

Satan then places his foot with a crushing impact upon Dr. Lawn's back. "UGH! YOU'RE CRUSHING ME!"

I'm going to do more than *that* to you before I'm through."

A firm voice interjects from behind. "I think you are through *NOW*!"

Satan quickly turns and is faced by Lucifer, Adam and Eve. Shocked at the confrontation of what was once *himself* a countless number of years ago, he shouts, "WHAT are you doing HERE?"

Lucifer observes and examines the entity called Satan and is appalled by the fact that what he sees is what *he* could become. The very sight sickens him to his stomach. "Are you.... Are *you* really that which I could be?"

"NO! I am that which you *will* be."

With an already awakening motherly nature within Eve, she instinctively runs to the badly injured Dr. Lawn to see how she could comfort him.

In shame and sadness, Lucifer addresses Satan: "If you are the source of all the uneasy and evil feelings I receive as well as all that which Lawn once shared with me, then you are surely wrong. I will _not_ become what you are now."

"You have _no_ choice. It is your **_DESTINY_**!"

Lucifer looks at Dr. Lawn with remorse. "I am sorry, my friend. Adam had explained to me what you had told him. It is now obvious to me that myself of the future, Satan, had deceived us both. At the time, I sensed something strange, but only thought it was the same spiritual elements I had felt from you earlier. Forgive me. _I_ should have known better. So close I came to repeating the fall with my Master's daughter, Eve. Shortly after I met Adam today, I once again felt that strange sense, but this time with great intensity. I knew it could not have come from you. After Adam explained what happened, I then knew it could only have been the evil one you told me about, _Satan_, the great deceiver of all."

"You flatter me," said Satan.

"YOU SHOULD BE ASHAMED AND DISGRACED, NOT FLATTERED," responded Lucifer, angrily. "_WE_ ARE THE CAUSE OF _ALL_ SUFFERING. _WE_ ARE THE DESTROYERS OF A BEAUTIFUL WORLD ORIGINALLY PLANNED. WE BEGAN IT ALL. NOW, _WE_ MUST END IT."

"What are you saying?" asked Satan.

"I am saying, dear predecessor, that it _is_ over. I am ending it _here_ and _now_. My position is that of a servant, and serve my Master faithfully I will. For Adam and Eve, his children, I will also serve them, as well."

"It is _done_, Satan," interjected Adam. "Soon, you will _no longer_ be Satan, but the angel Lucifer as it was always meant to be, in the bosom of God."

"_BULL SHIT!_ You think because _you_, Lucifer, decided to spare Eve your royal dick, that this will save all of you? You forget. _God_ is _POWERLESS_ now. He can do _NOTHING_. _I'm_ in charge now. _I_ say what goes. The great creator of all this shit can give you _no_ help. You're all on your own now, and if you can defeat _me_, _then_ and _only_ then do you win. NOW KNEEL, ALL OF YOU, _KNEEL_ BEFORE _YOUR_ MASTER."

"SATAN, DO NOT DO THIS, NOT _NOW_," answered Lucifer.

"KNEEL, I SAID. _KNEEL_!"

With the thrash of his hand, bolting energy sparks come flying out, forcing Adam, Eve and Lucifer to their knees. The clouds darken. The sound of morbid chants fill the air. The stench of decay overcomes even the fish in the sea. Death is all around. Evil is becoming stronger. Hope is becoming weaker…. In desperation, Dr. Lawn tries to stand by whatever power is left in him.

Satan lashes out at Lawn: "_YOU_! YOU ARE THE CAUSE OF THIS REBELLION." With a sinister laugh and grin, "BUT NOW, YOU'LL KNOW THE _FULL_ WRATH AND TERROR OF YOUR ONE AND _ONLY_ GOD, _ME_."

Dr. Lawn is then hurled away from Eve onto his back. As he attempts to straighten, he looks up and begins to see all forms of demonic spirits around himself. Then, he hears and sees all the horrors of thousands of years before him. As this occurs, he actually begins to feel each one, now crying and yelling out in agony. Lucifer, Adam and Eve, still on their knees, attempt to stand so they could help a tortured Dr. Lawn, but Satan's force is too powerful for them. Harder and harder they struggle, but to no avail. They must watch in utter horror as their friend begins to reach his pinnacle of pain.

Lucifer pleads with Satan: "STOP IT. STOP IT, SATAN! PLEASE, HAVE MERCY!"

"MERCY, YOU SAY. GOD SHOWED _ME_ NO MERCY WHEN ALL I WANTED TO DO WAS RECEIVE HIS LOVE."

"BUT NOW IS YOUR CHANCE," said Adam.

"I HAVEN'T HEARD FROM _YOU_, EVE. WHAT DO _YOU_ THINK?"

Tenderly.... "I almost fell in love with you because I _thought_ you were close to Heavenly Father, and I felt sorry for you. _Now_, as Satan, I can only have _hate_ and _contempt_. Please, show me the warmth I once knew," she said.

"WARMTH, WARMTH? I'LL SHOW YOU WARMTH."

Suddenly Dr. Lawn's body becomes red, as if burning inflames. His screams pierce all ears. In agony, he cries, "God! WHERE ARE YOU? HELP US, PLEASE FATHER."

"Forget Him. You're all _alone_ now. DENY HIM, _NOW_!"

"_NO_! I WON'T," cries Dr. Lawn.

Just then, Eve breaks loose of the grip and attacks Satan. But, with one blow of the arm, he sends her crashing to the ground in tears.

"HE HATES YOU! HE LAUGHS IN YOUR FACE. DENY HIM!" shouts Satan.

"*NO*! I *WON'T*," insists Dr. Lawn.

Then, Lucifer becomes free and engages in a short battle with Satan, but finally he, too, is flung to the ground, spiritually bound.

"THIS IS YOUR FINAL CHANCE. DENY GOD OR *PERISH*," cries Satan.

"*NO*! I LOVE HIM!" answers Lawn.

At this point, the Earth begins to shake and the winds reach high velocity as Adam is able to stand and create a force of energy of his *own*. As Satan sees this, he approaches Adam.

"I have *reigned* for all these years. Nothing or no one has ever been able to defeat me, not even the mighty armies of *God*, himself. I have *crushed* them all, as I will now *crush you*."

Now begins the final battle in history, as either man wins or Satan; good or evil; heaven or hell…. With all his force, Adam attacks Satan with a barrage of fists as a child would a big school bully. Satan just laughs and retaliates with lightning strikes of his own. Surely, such an inexperienced one such as Adam could *never* defeat one so great and powerful as Satan, or at least this is what goes through Satan's mind. As the fight continues, Adam becomes weaker and weaker, as Satan becomes stronger and stronger. As

Adam forces a weakened blow toward Satan, with one hand Satan picks him up by the chin in a final feeling of triumph.

His eyes vicious red and glaring, Satan says: "This is the _end_ now, you trash. I WIN! I HAVE WON!"

A battered Dr. Lawn now stands up and says "NO SATAN, YOU _LOSE_!"

Then, as in a planned unison, all the elements begin to erupt in fiery anger. The Earth's trembling gets worse and the skies explode. The agonizing cries of souls long forgotten echo together in harmony. The outer layers of Earth's atmosphere turn colors and quake in a deafening explosion. Everything becomes enveloped in a blaze of destruction. Everyone trembles where they stand. Even the mighty _Satan_ has been struck with fear. Suddenly, an enormous yell shrieks from Satan…. "NOOOOOOOOOOOOO"

All is quiet for quite some time. Then, Adam and Eve, Lucifer and Dr. Lawn manage to their feet, each without bodily harm or scars. The Earth is now as it was before Satan's dominion; calm, peaceful, joyous and beautiful. As the four gather together, they're stunned to see a tired and defeated Satan, lying on the ground. As they approach him, he utters his last words. Looking up with pathetic eyes, "So long I reigned. So long, only me. How could a few mortals defeat me? _How_ was it possible?"

Dr. Lawn answered him: "Because _God_ never gave up on us. He was _always_ here, waiting for us to give _Him_ the chance to work. _Once_ He _had_ the opportunity, then every existing entity _knew_ He was alive, _and_ working in all His glorious power. He _is_ our one and only God!"

"Where do I go from here?" asked Satan.

"Back to where you would have been if you had never fallen. Back to the angel Lucifer, loved servant of our Master," explained Lucifer.

As he looked up to the heavens, Satan exclaimed: "AS IT WAS WRITTEN, IT _IS_ DONE. _YOU HAVE WON!_"

Almost with a peacefulness, Satan lays down his head in the grass and closes his eyes. A soft breeze blows through the Garden as the spiritual body of Satan turns to dust and evaporates. The spiritual walls crumble, now, and all the tormented spirits and souls are free. A change begins. Liberation is here. Mankind and creation are saved, for the evil and the ancient Deceiver, _Satan_, are finally _dead_.

After a few minutes of contemplation and silent prayer, Adam, Eve, Lucifer and Dr. Lawn look up into the sky to see the last of the 3 doves fly by. The victory is definitely complete.

"That was the 3rd test. Complete faith in God, our Father," said Dr. Lawn.

"Three times you had to testify your faith in Father by not denying him, even under great pain and torture," said Eve. "The 3rd time sealed God's condition to save all his creation against Satan."

After a short while, Dr. Lawn turns to the other three, and with a serene voice, says "It _really_ is over now. No more sorrow; no more pain; no more tears; we did it together. My only regret is, when I leave for the new world, I will never remember any of this, or _you_."

"We will always be in your heart, my brother, as you in ours," said Adam. "Now there _is_ time for emotions."

A flood of tears cover the four of them as they all embrace, each understanding the other's heart….. 15 minutes later, Dr. Lawn bids his farewell with an aching heart. "I'm glad I had a chance to know the _real_ you, Lucifer. Good bye, Adam, Eve. I'm _proud_ to be your descendant. May the spirit of God always be with us all."

Dr. Lawn walks away to the stream he once bathed in when first arriving in the Garden. He quietly says, under his breath: "Kathy, Quint, Lieutenant Crane, I hope you are all in peace now, my friends. _We_ have done it. The shame is gone…. I am ready, now. I am ready to go."

One final time for Dr. Lawn, all becomes blank…… We now focus on the conversation of two people, sometime in the future…

While walking along a beach during sunrise, Lawn says, "Beautiful, isn't it Kathy? It never ceases to amaze me, the extent of Father's care and love for us."

"You're right, Frank," replies Peters. "I, too, am amazed. Just think. In a few days, man will have his first flight to another galaxy…. Did you ever wonder what it would be like if our original parents, Adam and Eve, had disobeyed Father instead of….."

"Why wonder about what never was," says Lawn as the two stop and face the rising sun behind the ocean. "Let's just enjoy the magic of this moment, and what *is*. It's the dawn of a brand new day."

As the sun begins to glimmer upon the ocean, sea gulls glide through the air, whining with a different tone, this time, for they fly with pride and joy in their hearts. It is great to be alive, *because* of man, not in spite of him. This *is* a new day. This *is* a brand new world.

Made in the USA
Columbia, SC
15 December 2017